ALICE AND THE RUBY QUEEN SQUARED

Minecraft Fairy Tale Series

By: Tom Garzan & Z. Willingham & M.C. Ostberg

D1521501

TABLE OF CONTENTS

INTRODUCTION

Welcome to the Minecraft Fairy Tales

Series! Through these books you will

explore the classic tales – with a twist. A

Minecraft twist! Travel through the world of

fantasy with these tales that will captivate

you until the end!

PART ONE

Follow That Pig

Once upon a time, there lived a girl named Alice who loved to read books. She read so much and so often that her parents worried she would never get out of her head and into the real world. They tried to make sure she spent a lot of time with her big sister, all in the hopes that Elizabeth would help make Alice see the fun in the real world.

Elizabeth was secretly a lover of books, too. So, each day when she and Alice would go out on their walks, they would hide books in their pockets and find a tree safely out of sight of the house and sit down to read.

It was a normal day like this when Elizabeth fell asleep while they were reading. It was a bright and clear summer day with the smell of the grass and flowers in the air. Perfect for reading.

Alice was deep into a classic fairy tale by the Grimm's Brothers when she heard a noise on the other side of the tree she was leaning against. She ignored it at first, so deep in her book she did not want to look, but after a third time hearing the *oink,* she knew she had to see.

Crawling around the tree on her knees – careful not to dirty her dress or her mother would be upset – Alice spotted a pig on the edge of a large hole in the ground.

The pig was square.

"Curious," said Alice. "A square pig where no pig should exist. What are you doing, little square pig?"

The pig looked directly at Alice, oinked and then jumped in the hole!

"Mr. Pig! Where are you going?" Alice was definitely curious about this pig now. Crawling closer to the hole, she felt the earth start to give way as she leaned over to see if the pig was okay. Just as she realized it was crumbling too fast and that she had leaned too far, she fell.

Alice let out a scream as the air rushed by her, making her hair fly. She saw that it was light in the hole, despite falling so deep.

It seemed like ages she fell and she started to get bored almost.

Many things were falling with her, though she saw no sign of the square pig. Strangely, everything that fell was square as well. Plates, chairs, clocks and even large blue diamonds.

Looking down towards the bottom of the hole, Alice caught a glimpse of her legs. They were turning square, too! She quickly brought her arms into her view and saw they were square! Reaching up, she felt her head turning from round to square as she held it. She was a block person!

"Oh, dear. Oh, dear!" Alice was very worried now.

After what seemed like ages, Alice finally saw what looked like the bottom of the hole in sight. Breathing a sigh of relief, Alice closed her eyes, expecting to fall hard on the ground. Instead, she landed on what felt like a soft pillow. Opening her eyes, she saw light everywhere. It was so bright after the darker hole that it took her a minute for her eyes to adjust.

Once her vision had cleared, she saw that she *had* landed on a pillow. All around her was green grass, trees and blue sky, just like at home. Except that everything was made out of square blocks.

"What is this strange place?" Alice asked aloud, hoping for an answer.

She turned around in a circle and it was then she noticed the teapot. Not an ordinary teapot, but a huge one that looked like a house. It had tea coming out of it like a waterfall and it was falling into a huge teacup. Everything was so large and still made up of square blocks.

Alice walked over to the teacup and looked up at the waterfall. It was a real one for sure, but it did not seem to get her wet like the ones in her world. It even smelled like nice sweet tea. It also barely splashed anywhere.

"Would you like some?" A voice from behind startled Alice.

She turned to see a young man dressed very strangely. Not only was he square like Alice now was, he was wearing a suit of crazy colors and the most bizarre hat Alice had ever seen. It had birds, flowers and even a small tree on it – but they were all make out of tiny square blocks.

The man cleared his throat and asked again, "Would you like some?"

"I'm sorry, I didn't mean to be rude," Alice said shyly. "Yes, I would love some."

The man pointed to the other side of the teapot house where Alice saw a real picnic table set up with a full tea service. Walking over, she realized how difficult it was to move with a square body. Getting used to this would take a lot of time.

After they were seated, Alice said, "Thank you. My name is Alice."

"You're welcome. I am Mad Cap. This is my home in Minecraft."

"What is Minecraft?"

"Why it is the world you have fallen into, my dear Alice." Mad Cap seemed a strange sort, almost like the types of silly characters that Alice read in her fairy tale books.

"Please choose one, Alice." Mad Cap pointed to a teacup and a small cake on the table.

"I don't understand." The entire new world was confusing to Alice. There was so much to take in at once.

"If you aren't sure, I would suggest you try the cake first."

Alice looked closer at the cake and saw that it had *Eat Me* written in red sprinkles on it. What an unusual way to decorate a cake. Taking a very small piece, she placed it on her tongue and immediately felt…different. While this feeling was coming over her, Mad Cap started talking fast.

"You are here for a reason, Alice. You know all the tales and all the ways to defeat the Ruby Queen. I am sorry I had to trick you, but that was the only way." Mad Cap truly looked sad that he had to trick her. "Eating a tiny piece of this cake will turn you into a skeleton. That is a monster in Minecraft, who has the powerful skill of shooting deadly arrows. Skeletons guard the Queen only, so this was the only way to get you close to her. The drink here," he gestured to the small bottle labeled *Drink Me*, "will turn you back into your normal self in Minecraft."

Alice tried to talk, but it was too late. She could already feel the change happening, and before her eyes, her body lost its clothing and skin as she turned into bones.

PART TWO

A Bone to Pick

"We need you to be our savior, Alice. Queen Ruby is taking over our world and killing it. She threatens the entire Overworld falling to the dark forces of the Netherworld. I need you to travel across the Overworld and get into the Queen's throne room and shoot her with this enchanted bow." He placed a brown quiver and bow on the table in front of her. "Queen Ruby's sister, Princess Lily, will take over this world and

20

protect us from the Netherworld and Minecraft monsters from taking over."

Alice was confused, but her heart went out to this world that obviously needed a hero. Though she was young, she hoped she could help them. It was like living in a real fairy tale! She had learned all kinds of tricks from reading her books and she hoped they would come in handy now.

She nodded to Mad Cap and took the bow and quiver, placing both on her back. Just as she was about to leave, he reminded her about the bottle of *Drink Me* to turn her back to herself.

"You may take as many sips and bites as you need. I might suggest you practice changing back and forth a few times to understand how it feels and how long it takes. When traveling in our world, you will face many dangers. You might be safer in skeleton form."

Alice put the bottle into her quiver and gave Mad Cap a small bow of understanding.

"Wait!" Mad Cap yelled out as Alice started to walk away. "You will need a map. The Overworld is divided into four parts with a circle square in the center. Each part has its own gate to get into the Main Circle. I have given you a key to get out of this world and into the Queen's world. Do not lose them. They are very hard to get and it is my only set."

Alice nodded again and took the map. Walking away from Mad Cap, she felt a bit scared, but she knew her mission and how much she wanted to succeed, especially now that she had the opportunity to become a hero. She was excited to get her chance after many years of reading about them in her fairy tale books.

She walked for nearly an hour, taking time to shoot at the trees and practice her aim. She was surprised when she found that her quiver held unlimited arrows and she would not have to stop to gather them. Once she had shot twenty trees in a row, she decided it was time to change back into herself. Taking out the *Drink Me* bottle, she opened it and sniffed. It did not smell strange. It smelled like apples actually.

Taking a small sip, she felt the change coming and corked the bottle tight, placing it back in her quiver for safekeeping. Within minutes, she saw her body start to change. It started with her feet and crept up her body in a steady wave. Her legs, arms and head all of a sudden popped into a square shape.

Alice started walking around in a circle to get the feel of moving with her new body shape. It took a few minutes, but she was able to stride normally once she got the hang of it.

Taking out the map Mad Cap had given her, she studied where she should go. There were four worlds on the map around the Main Circle: Village World, Ruby Land, Monster Land and Netherworld. Alice saw she was in Village World now. Ruby Land was directly across the Main Circle from here with Netherworld on her left and Monster Land on her right.

She tried to see if there was any other way to get to Ruby Land than going into the

Main Circle, but after studying the map for a few minutes, she realized it was the fastest and only way to get to the Queen's castle in Ruby Land.

Alice started walking again and after an hour, she saw what looked like a black and purple doorway. It had purple squares surrounded by black squares. There were no steps, just what looked like the doorway and no fence on either side.

Alice decided to test to see if she could go around the gate. No matter where she tried to walk through on either side of the gate, an invisible wall pushed her back.

"How weird. I guess I will have to go through the gate then."

Dumping out her quiver, she looked at the items Mad Cap gave to her. There were four small blocks, all in different colors: green, red, white and gray, like a mossy stone. She also had her *Eat Me* cake and *Drink Me* bottle. The last thing was a small hand-written note.

The note said:

Alice, these are your keys to get through the gates. To use them, tap the block in front of the gate, the gate will disappear, and you can walk through. The gate will come back once you are through, so do not leave the key on the wrong side. We are counting on you, Alice. Best of luck.

Mad Cap

Looking at the map again, she saw that the green block went to Village World, the red to Ruby Land, the white to Netherworld and the gray to Monster Land.

Once she had this sorted, she picked up the green stone and put the others back in her quiver. She was about to put the bottle and cake back in as well when she thought that perhaps she should turn into a skeleton since she didn't know what to expect on the other side of the gate.

Taking a small bite of the cake, she felt herself start to change. Within moments, she looked down and saw she was in skeleton form. Her long, boney fingers flexed as she put the items back in and placed her quiver on her back.

Tapping the green block, she walked through the space where the portal was and then looked around at the Main Circle.

PART THREE

Friends in Strange Places

The Main Circle was... well, a circle. It was the size of three football fields in any direction. It had a red and white checkerboard ground with trees placed around it and with benches underneath. Alice looked to her left and could see the gate for Monster Land. There were several monsters banging on it and the invisible fence on the sides of the gate to try to get through.

Some were green with black eyes and, of course, a square body. Some looked like dead villagers who had been turned into zombies. None of them was able to get through, but closer to the side of the gate, Alice saw there was a slime-type monster who was able to ooze through the small gap. They were green and blobby and seemed to be in a variety of different sizes from small to medium to large.

Alice heard grunting and looked to her right to see a large, tan metal creature fighting the slime that had already gotten through. He looked almost like a robot. He took his large fists and smashed the slime to bits anytime it got close to him. Once he smashed them, the globs went everywhere but did not reform. Just melted into the ground.

Walking over to this creature, Alice felt confident that he was a good person. He just had that look. She decided to take a sip of the *Drink Me* to change back into herself while she watched him defeat the slime.

Once she was herself again, she asked, "Do you need some help?"

The creature turned to her and looked at her as if she were crazy. "Of course not! I'm the bravest and strongest of the iron golems in the Overworld."

Iron golem? Alice thought to herself, having no clue what that meant, but assumed that was what type of creature he was. She shrugged her square shoulders and watched him continue to beat the slime until all near him was gone.

"I'm Alice." She stood there waiting for the iron golem to respond.

He looked her up and down and said, "My God, a human! What are you doing here?"

"I fell into a hole after chasing a square pig. I met the Mad Cap and he sent me on a mission to save the Overworld from Queen Ruby. I have a cake to change me into a skeleton to be able to defeat her."

"You want to defeat the Ruby Queen?" He did not look like he believed her at first, but after a minute, he decided she must be the savior they had all heard would come one day. "She killed all my brothers and used their parts to make a giant fan to fan herself when she gets too hot. My name is Cobalt and I'll help you with whatever you need."

"Thank you. I think I'm going to need all the help I can get in this strange new world."

Alice shook his hand and they both turned to look across the Main Circle to the Ruby Land gate.

"If I may offer a suggestion," Cobalt offered hesitantly. "We should check out the other gates to make sure they are secure before we move on. Did you come through the Village World gate?"

"Yes, Mad Cap gave me a key for all of them."

"Great, then we know that one is secure. The Monster Land gate has been breached, but I do not see Queen Ruby doing anything about that anytime soon. Let's go check out the Netherworld gate to make sure."

"Sounds smart. You lead the way, Cobalt," Alice said with relief at having a friend in this weird new world.

After a few minutes of walking, they could see the Netherworld gate in the distance. Right outside the gate was a floating…thing… that looked like a ball of flame. The ball of fire was shooting its own fireballs at the gate.

"What in the world is that?" Alice was a bit scared, but also very interested in this unusual new creature.

"What in the tic, tac, tock... Hey! What are you doing there?" Cobalt obviously recognized the type of creature and did not like what he was seeing.

The flamed ball jumped in the air and turned quickly, shooting a fireball at Alice and Cobalt. They managed to duck just in time.

"What was that for?" Alice was no longer curious. She was angry at almost been burnt to a crisp.

"I'm so sorry. I did not mean to do that. I just wanted to get home and you startled me." Shocked that the ball of fire could talk, Alice's mouth hung open. Then she looked closer and saw tears. The fireball was *crying*.

"What are you doing here on this side of the gate? And what do you mean get home?" Cobalt was not moved by the tears and wanted answers.

"I escaped from Queen Ruby and now I just want to get back to my parents and sisters, but I can't get through the gate. I fear I am lost to them and will be stuck in this circle forever." The fireball sobbed even more.

Alice's heart melted at the sight of such a fearsome creature in her world crying in this one. "Well, we are going to defeat the Queen and you can come with us if you'd like."

"Really? That might be the only way to get me home. Do you promise to help me once you defeat the Ruby Queen?"

"Yes, of course. I always keep my promises."

"Deal. My name is Blaze and I would be happy to help you." Blaze stuck his fiery hand out from his ball-shaped body and once Alice saw that Cobalt could touch it without getting hurt, she shook it herself. It was odd how his fire body did not burn her human skin.

Now that the group was all agreed in their desired plan, they started to move towards the final gate, the Ruby Land gate, where Queen Ruby's castle was.

Once they came close, they noticed a square horse standing on the wrong side of the gate. He looked very frustrated, but had a beautiful brown coat. Alice wanted to pet him, but the horse shied away as soon as she started to get close.

Looking in her quiver, she tried to see if she had something she could use to tempt the horse closer. Spotting an apple, she pulled it out and offered it to the animal.

"For me, my dear? Thank you!" the horse said and sucked up the apple in one bite.

"Oh…*crunch, crunch*…this is lovely…*slurp*...I've been so hungry since I was kicked out of the castle."

Alice stared in amazement at the talking horse.

"Thank you, my dear. Whatever are you doing here? You are a human!" The horse had finished the apple and now went on to question Alice.

Alice shared a glance with Blaze and Cobalt, who both nodded in agreement in trusting this horse. "I'm here on a mission after falling through a hole. I have been tasked with helping to save your world from Queen Ruby."

"Save our world how?" Crazily, the horse raised his eyebrow in disbelief.

"By defeating the Ruby Queen."

PART FOUR

Into the Unknown

"Well, in that case, then I will help you as well. That woman has taken my son, Brony the Pony, to use as her personal footrest."

"That sounds great, but what are you doing here?" asked Alice.

"Once she saw that I was too old to hold her feet up and couldn't move as fast, she took my son and had her skeletons push me out of the gate. I cannot get back in and I just want to rescue my son. Will you help me?" The horse pleaded with such big eyes that Alice's heart melted again and she agreed on the spot.

"Yes, if you help us defeat the Ruby Queen, then we will help you rescue your son. By the way, this is Cobalt and Blaze; they are helping me on this quest, too." Alice pointed out the huge iron golem and the small fireball.

"Nice to meet you. I'm Winston."

"Glad to have you on board," said Cobalt.

"So, how do we get through the gate then?" asked Blaze.

"Simple," Alice said as she took off her quiver. "I have a key." She reached in and pulled out the small red square block. Once she tapped the top of the block, the gate magically disappeared. The others stood there with stunned expressions on their faces.

"Where'd you get that?" Blaze asked, amazed.

"Mad Cap gave me it to get through the gate. I only have one, though." Alice did not want to reveal that she had keys to all the worlds. She was afraid the others would not help her if they thought they could get home without helping her.

The quartet walked through the gate, Alice the last to step through. Once she did, the small red block shook and the gate magically appeared again.

The first thing they saw up the path was a checkpoint manned by a duo of skeletons.

Alice pulled the group to the side behind a square clump of trees and bushes. "Look, I don't want to scare you all, but I have a cake that will turn me into a skeleton. Mad Cap gave it to me so that I can pretend to be one to get close to the queen. If I take it now, I can turn and then I can pretend that I captured you all and lead you into the castle with no issues." Alice pulled the cake out. "I'm going to take a bite and turn now. *Do not* scream or we will be caught."

Taking a small bite, Alice felt herself shift into the now-familiar form. The others jumped back in surprise, but she grunted and put her hands up to remind them it was just her. She directed the group to follow her up the path and they walked up the checkpoint.

Once she got there, Alice took a chance and tried to talk like normal, hoping it comes out in skeleton talk. She pounded her skeleton hand on her chest, pointed to the prisoners, and grunted. The guards got excited and repeated the chest pound, allowing her to pass through with her captives.

The group of heroes started walking up the path towards the trees. After they came through a large clump of forest, they saw a huge castle. It was done all in red stone with fluffy white clouds as the roof. Huge flamingos, instead of posts, supported the entrance and held up the building.

They all stopped and stared at the ridiculousness of it all.

"What are the clouds for?" asked Cobalt.

"So the queen can control the weather in her castle whenever she wants," says Winston.

"How silly! Why would she want that?" laughed Cobalt.

"Because she wants what she wants when she wants it. She is a greedy woman. That's all." Blaze said this with a brightening of his fire and looked ready to shoot a fireball.

Alice grunted to Cobalt and gestured with her hand towards to the castle. Noticing the idea of what she meant, Cobalt asked,

"Ok, Winston, you know this place. Where do we go from here to get access to the queen?"

Winston stopped and thought a moment, tapping his front hooves on the ground. "We need to get to the throne room. The Queen spends most of her days there having villagers come in and dance for her. If they don't dance to her liking, she has the skeletons push them out the gates or into the dungeon."

"Well, that seems easy enough. Can you lead us Winston?" asked Blaze.

"Yes, but remember – I'm not supposed to be here and we are here as Alice's captives. We should be sent to the throne room right away, anyway, to dance for the Queen and have her decide our fate."

Alice grunted again and started to lead the way. She took them up the steps with them following in line behind her. Winston was directly behind her, whispering directions so that they could navigate the castle.

The whole castle was a mishmash of winding hallways filled with all manner of ridiculousness.

On one wall was a portrait of a sad clown. On another was the skin of an animal that was all different rainbow colors. On the tables, there were strange knickknacks all in square shapes. Alice could just make out a spoon left in a bowl of ice cream that had molded over. It was disgusting, yet it was in a decorative box as if it was art.

They moved through the hallways cautiously with Alice wanting so badly to open doors and look in the rooms they passed to see more of this crazy world. However, she did not because she knew her mission was important to the people of this world.

As they approached a large set of doors, they saw four skeletons, two on each side, guarding them.

Alice grunted and pointed to her captives. The skeletons took turns opening the massive doors. It took them almost five minutes to open them with all four skeleton guards pulling at once.

Once they were open, the group entered the throne room with Alice in the lead. They were all inside when they realized that the Queen was sitting on her throne.

PART FIVE

The Ruby Queen Squared

Alice was shocked to see that the Ruby Queen was human. Though she was block shaped, she had obviously been human at one point.

Queen Ruby had gorgeous long blonde hair and she was wearing a red gown covered in rubies. The gown was so heavy she could barely sit up straight on her throne with all the weight.

Alice walked closer and then froze in place.

She knew this queen.

Thank goodness, she could not talk as a skeleton. Otherwise, she would have yelled out a name.

Aunt Scarlett? Alice thought.

The Ruby Queen was Alice's Aunt Scarlett who had been missing for seven years in the real world. It looked as though she was not missing anymore.

Queen Ruby – or Aunt Scarlett – called Alice forward with her prisoners.

"Come forward, Skeleton. I need entertainment!"

Alice saw a mad gleam in her aunt's eye and realized that her aunt had gone insane during her time in Minecraft. She must have fallen into a hole the same way Alice had.

Alice wondered if Mad Cap had planned all this because she was the Queen's niece.

They group walked forward and Alice directed Cobalt to go first.

Cobalt started break dancing, but he was so rusty from fighting the slime that all he did was make huge screeching noises every time he moved.

The Queen got angry and red in the face at this noise and said, "No, no, *no*! That will not do! Off with him!" Then she screamed at Alice, "Next!"

Alice pushed Blaze forward, safe from his fire now because she was dead as a skeleton.

Blaze started juggling fireballs. He was so scared, though, he dropped one and it scorched the floor. The Queen screamed, "NO, NO, NO! You have ruined my beautiful floor! Get the water." She directed this last part to her servant next to her, ordering them to go leave and get the water. "Next!" she yelled.

Winston knew it was his time and nodded to Alice to give her to signal to be ready to shoot the Queen.

Alice nodded back in understanding.

Winston stepped forward and the Queen gasped. "Winston! What are you doing here? Have you come to try to get your son back? Well, you aren't getting him," the Queen sneered at the brave brown horse.

Winston looked down at the queen's feet and saw his purple son, Brony, there with a pained face as the Queen's heels dug into his back.

"I don't need your permission to get him back." With these words, Winston nodded to Alice and Alice pulled out an arrow and shot at the Queen.

Once she saw the Queen fall, Alice took a quick drink of the *Drink Me* and turned back into herself. She rushed over to her aunt and hugged her to her chest. "Aunt Scarlett. It's me, Alice."

Scarlett reached up, touched Alice's face, and said, "My dear Alice. Have you come to rescue me and finally take me home?"

"Yes," said Alice with a tear in her eye.

Just as it looked like Scarlett was fading, a black void opened up and swallowed Alice and Scarlett.

Alice woke up next to the tree where she had been reading before she fell into Minecraft. She looked across the yard and saw her Aunt Scarlett hugging her mother and sister.

Walking over to them, Alice's mother said, "Look, Alice! Your Aunt Scarlett has returned." Then turning back to her sister, Alice's mother said, and "I want to hear all about your tales from the last seven years of travelling the world, my dear sister."

Scarlett smiled down at her younger sister and then turned to Alice and winked.

PART SIX

Happily Ever After

The White Queen, Queen Lily, soon took over the Overworld and set all to right. The monsters were kept in Monster Land and the villagers had security from invading monsters by allowing a standing army of iron golems to patrol their villages.

Village World prospered as new villagers moved back in now that things were safer. Netherworld stayed the same with their own ruler and their own creatures. None passed into the Main Circle or the other worlds without permission from Queen Lily.

The Queen even redid the entire castle. It was done in white stone with a normal roof. The flamingos that had held the place of stone pillars were set free to live a happy life. They were replaced with gorgeous carved stone pillars. There were four and they were carved in the shape of an iron golem, a horse, a fireball and a human girl to honor the four who had saved their world.

Cobalt became head of the new Queen's security. He hired an entire guard of iron golems to protect the realm and now had a completely new set of brothers. After a few months, the Queen surprised him. She had the royal engineer rebuild his brothers so that he could be reunited with his family.

Blaze returned home to his family in the Netherworld and met another fireball. They are now happily raising baby fireballs in a small lava pool there. Blaze brings his family regularly to come visit his friends and his Queen, as the royal ambassador from the Netherworld.

Winston and his son, Brony, were given to a villager in the Village World named Alex. They now live a comfortable life, eating hay, playing and frolicking in the tulip fields all day long.

Alice grew up to be an amazing writer. She told stories of this mysterious world she visited as a child. Now, she lives in a huge castle-like house that is in no way red or pink.

Aunt Scarlett returned to normal and kept up the secret of her seven-year disappearance by explaining that she had traveled the world. She went on to actually travel the world after being in Minecraft for so long. She still was afraid of anything square shaped and lived in a roundhouse where everything, even the bed and sink, was round.

The End

ABOUT THE AUTHORS

Tom Garzan

Tom Garzan loves all things Minecraft and fairy tales. At his children's urging, he combined his love of both into this exciting new series. He currently lives in the Northeastern U.S. with his 5 children, wife, 2 dogs, 14 chickens, 2 rabbits, a goat and a rather rude pig. He is excited to bring you a whole new way of reading fairy tales!

Facebook:

https://www.facebook.com/authortomgarzan

/

Find free audio versions on the Minecraft

Fairy Tales YouTube Channel:

https://www.youtube.com/channel/UC5qza

K3sw1Gbor3kcEkT2LA

Z. Willingham

Z. Willingham is a seventh grader with a passion for Minecraft and reading. He plays it daily, much to his mother's insanity. Now becoming a teenager, he has decided it is time to go to work and help his friend, Tom Garzan, to write these awesome Minecraft stories.

M.C. Ostberg

M.C. Ostberg is a teenager with a plan – a Minecraft plan. Going to school by day and playing Minecraft by night, he has built up a massive amount of worlds in the game. He is using his skills to help Tom Garzan develop realistic Minecraft books that all kids will love.

Other Books in the Series

Steve and the Seven Iron Golems

Steve is a prince who has a charmed life, but when his father dies, his mother is forced to marry the evil Duke Herobrine. Herobrine takes over the kingdom after Steve's mother passes as well and Steve is forced to be a servant to him for ten years. When Steve finally has a chance to escape, he finds friends in a group of seven iron golems. But Herobrine has other plans and poisons Steve. Knowing the only way to save him is to find his true love, the seven golems embark to find her. Can Steve be awoken in time to reclaim his crown and take over as the rightful ruler of the Overworld? Find out now inside!

Alice and the Ruby Queen Squared

Alice is an ordinary girl in an ordinary world when one day she sees a square pig and follows it down a dark, deep hole. Now, I know this story sounds familiar, but it is anything but! When she lands, she finds she is in world full of blocks. Everything is square - including her. After meeting with a strange man named Mad Cap, she is told she was brought here to save the Overworld from the evil Queen Ruby. She is given specific items that will help her on her quest. Armed with a magic cake and drink.

Alice ventures into this new world and picks up some friends along the way. Using her magic items, as well as her trusty bow and arrows, she makes her way into the world of Minecraft. Will Alice be able to defeat Queen Ruby and still make it home safe? Find out now inside!

Peter and the Skeleton Pirate

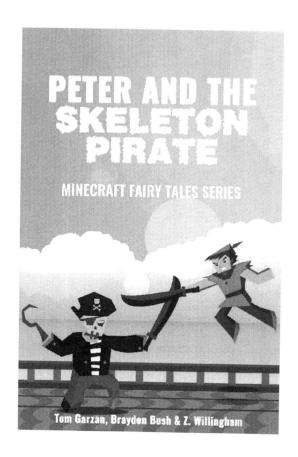

Peter and Tink are on their way home from a party

at the Darling house when Tink nods off. With

Peter left to navigate the way home and the sun

quickly rising, there is sure to be an issue. Seeing

four stars instead of two, Peter picks the wrong one

and ends up sending them spiraling into a vortex of

the unknown. What happens next includes a

skeleton pirate, some really dirty socks, a bunch of

large metal beats, a dainty burp and a group of

determined villagers. Will Peter and Tink be able

to help save the day AND make it back to

Neverland?

Hoody and the Cave Endermen

Hoody is an Enderman with a conscience. No longer enjoying stealing from the villagers, he tries to stand up to his fellow Endermen - only to be kicked out in the cold. Zaq is a young boy with a keen eye and knows something is happening with the village items that keep getting stolen. After a day in the woods, he comes across an Enderman who seems different. The two of them soon become the best of friends and team up together to help save the village from more thefts and to stop the evil Endermen from coming back. They have a plan, but can they really trap and all the Endermen and save the village? Find out now inside!

Alex is a girl who loves walking through the woods, kicking skeleton butt (or bones) and especially visiting her grandmother. But things have been changing in her little village. People are starting to act... strange. So she goes to check on her grandmother one day, wearing her thick red cloak against the cold. What she finds is something of her worst fears. Her grandmother is not the same as she used to be! Steve is a wizard who is down on his luck. No one will buy his potions and he is starting to doubt his abilities as a healer. Knowing of the zombie changes in the local villages, he has set out to make a potion that will cure those afflicted. The problem is he has no one to test it on. Will Alex, her grandmother and Steve find a way to cure all of their problems? Find out now inside!

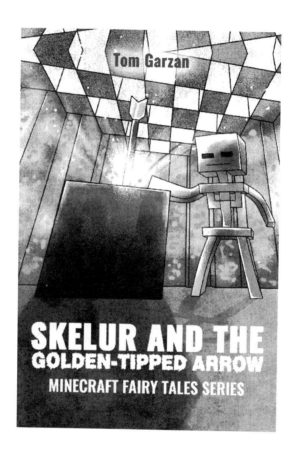

Skelur is a small, skinny skeleton with a big skull that gets picked on by everyone and is never allowed to go on raids. King Bonerot has tasked him with finding new villages to raid for food. After being given a mysterious prophecy by the Grand Elder, Skelur sets out on a journey that will change his life and the lives of all the skeletons in his village. Go along in this epic quest inside now!

Creepy is a cursed creeper, but he will never tell you what he is cursed with. He is so lonely. So when he finds a man trying to take one of his precious blue flowers, he wants nothing more than for him to stay with him and be his friend. But the man is afraid and Creepy isn't the best at convincing people to be his friend. Demanding he send him his daughter, he lets the man go.

Daisy is a girl unlike any other. Beloved by all, especially her father. She would do anything to make him happy and keep him safe. So when he is threatened by a creeper, she sacrifices herself by going to live in a scary castle deep in the woods.

Will Daisy survive the dangers that lurk in the castle? And will Creepy ever find the friend he so wants and cure his curse?

Made in the USA
Middletown, DE
06 August 2016